THE WIND

A STARLITE MYSTERY

THE STARLITE SUPERNATURAL MYSTERY SERIES

RAY & MICHELE FRASER

 Created with Vellum

*We dedicate this story to everyone who believes
in old wives' tales or has lived through
a bone chilling winter storm.*

ONE

Mike Wilson leaned hard into the wind. Forcing his way into the gale took a tremendous effort, and though he had traveled only a short distance, he had already begun to sweat profusely inside his down-filled coat.

He took a deep breath and trudged on. Someone had to endure the weather to get the medicine, he thought. If his daughter, Zoe, didn't get another dose soon, her fever would go back up. It was their only hope. The high winds and heavy, blinding snow dashed any hope that they would be able to get her to the hospital tonight.

The pharmacist, Earl Fisher, had agreed to meet Mike at the drugstore. Fortunately, there was enough medicine on hand to refill Zoe's prescription one more time, but it would only last two days. Hopefully, that would be long enough for the storm to cease and the crews to do their jobs. Clear roads would make it possible for Mike and his wife to take Zoe to the hospital in Lebanon, nearly thirty miles away.

Katie Wells, Zoe's doctor, had examined her and ran a complete series of tests. Nothing was conclusive; a slight fever, aches, pains, and some mild head congestion. Whatever was causing her illness, wasn't responding to any of the antibiotics that were normally used to treat colds and flu. Doc Wells had prescribed a rarely used drug that was designed to cover all the bases. At least for now, it seemed to be working.

Mike and Andrea needed time. Regardless of the origin of the infection, the drug was designed to curb its growth. That meant they had a little bit longer; time for the weather to break, for the roads to be cleared, and to get Zoe to the hospital for additional tests.

Mike pushed on. Only six more blocks to go. Canaan, New Hampshire is a small town in the upper quadrant of the state, nestled in the hills of the scenic north. Canaan takes you back to a setting reminiscent of the *Legend of Sleepy Hollow.*

In the spring, summer, and fall, it's a beautiful place to live. In the winter, it's often brutal, with constant snowfall and a wind that cuts through the spirit of even the hardiest souls.

The snow had turned to a sleet-like consistency, with the small ice crystals stinging Mike's face and neck. Canaan was not New York or Boston. Earl's pharmacy was the only one within twenty miles; people had nowhere else to go. Fortunately, Earl was a single man who took his work seriously. He had a room in the back of the drugstore where he occasionally slept when the weather got bad. He would sleep there tonight.

A well-running snowmobile is a necessity in the snowy Northeast. Mike owned one, but just before Zoe took ill, it quit running. Fortunately, the snow had not started falling in earnest and Mike was able to trailer it to Vince's Service Center. The news wasn't good. It needed an oil pump and the shop didn't have one in stock.

As a lifelong resident of Canaan, he knew the vehicle's importance. "I gotta order it from Concord, Mike. I should have it in a day or so. If I can get some of these other machines up and running while we wait for the part, I could have you back on the road in less than a week."

What Vince hadn't planned on was the snowstorm that blew in that very night. The heavy snow and blowing drifts made the roads into, or out of, Canaan, completely impassable.

At this time of year, Vince's Service Center was one of the busiest places in town. Vince was often seen working late into the night, doing his best to get the snowmobiles repaired and back in the hands of their owners.

Mike didn't want to think about what might happen if they had to wait a week to get Zoe to the hospital. Right now, the best thing he could do was be sure that Zoe had the medicine she needed to stop the spread of her infection, which meant a long trek through deep snow to the pharmacy.

A light in the distance flickering through the driving snow gave Mike a renewed burst of energy. The store was now only two blocks away. If Earl was true to form, he'd have a pot of hot coffee brewing to help warm them up and give Mike the strength to get back home.

The wind gusted strongly in his face. "Damn wind," he cursed, leaning further into the gale. Mike hoped that the wind would continue blowing in the same direction for his walk home. If it did, it would make his homeward trek easier.

"Hello, Mike. How's the little one?" Earl asked stepping back away from the door, and then closing it to the whistle of the wind once Mike had stepped through.

Mike loosened his coat and shook the snow off his parka. "Well, for now, she's holding her own. Doc says as long as her temperature stays down, she'll be fine for a while. They still can't figure out what's wrong with her, and they can't send the specimens to Lebanon for testing. We'll just have to wait for the weather to break." Earl nodded, handing Mike a steaming cup of coffee.

"Well, they say it should end by tomorrow evening. I know the crews are working full time to try and get the roads to the highway opened."

"That would be a miracle," Mike replied. "We're not frightened, but we are concerned. Doc says she hasn't got a clue. I just hope it's not because of the wind."

The aging pharmacist ran a thin hand through his silver hair. "Naw, don't you go believing that malarkey. That's just a tall tale. There's no truth to it."

Mike shrugged, "I sure hope you're right, Earl. You know there's a lot of people around here that wouldn't agree with you."

"I know, but just remember what I said - It's an old wives' tale."

Mike Wilson said nothing, he simply tipped the cup up and finished the last of his coffee before setting it on the counter. He zipped the inner lining of his parka and snapped his windbreaker securely. With the prescription bag in his pocket, he shook hands with Earl before putting his gloves on. "Thanks for being here and for the coffee, Earl."

"Any time, Mike."

The last trace of warmth faded quickly with

the closing of the pharmacy door behind him. Mike headed towards home. He shook his head, the wind still blowing in his face. It was as though it knew he had changed the direction that he was traveling.

"Damn wind," he groaned.

The wind in Canaan was different. It wasn't simply wind; it appeared to be almost sentient. Local folklore said that when the wind started blowing like this, some people disappeared and others died.

There was some history that supported this belief. Two years ago, when the wind was not nearly this bad, Wesley Anderson had simply vanished and was never found. The fact that he disappeared into thin air is not what made the story seem so odd. When they searched his home, his coat, hat, and boots were still there. In fact, there were no footprints in the deep snow that surrounded his house. He was just gone.

Six years ago, the wind gusted violently. When it had calmed, every member of the Clifton family had died of some mysterious ailment. Once Carol Clifton got sick, within a week all five members of the family had died. When they found their bodies, it looked as if they had merely gone to sleep. The doctors were never able to determine the actual cause of their deaths.

If the truth were to be known, Mike's real

fear was that somehow or other, Zoe had caught the same disease that claimed the Cliftons. When they passed away, the weather was very similar to what Canaan had been experiencing during the last week. Back then, the Cliftons also didn't have the opportunity to get Carol to the hospital.

Mike whispered a silent prayer. As the words of hope passed through his mind, the wind increased in intensity and quickly switched directions, blowing at Mike from behind and almost knocking him face down in the snow. *Some wives' tale*, he thought.

Mike's small home was now in view. He envisioned his wife watching out the window for his return, peering through the blinding snow to catch a glimpse of his orange windbreaker.

"Wretched wind," Mike muttered. "If you are evil, find someone else. Don't hurt my Zoe!"

As Mike spoke the last word, the wind once again gusted and assumed a howl. It continued, loud and persistent, sounding like it was being blown through a tunnel. Mike continued to walk, ignoring the wind's shrill whistle. The howl changed its repeating crescendo as if responding to his plea for Zoe.

At last, he stepped into the shelter of the porch on the front of his house, closing the door behind him. The moment the door latched the wind seemed to take a different tone, as if freeing him from its grasp.

"Are you okay?" Andrea, asked.

"Yeah. Mainly my feet are a little cold. The snow was too deep and kept filling my boots."

Andrea Wilson had reason to worry. She'd also lived in Canaan her whole life and saw many bad winters in her twenty-nine years. This one was different. There was an eeriness about it. Like Mike, she silently feared for Zoe and the others in their town.

Mike left his coat and boots in the mudroom, then stood warming himself in front of the fireplace. Andrea went to check on Zoe. When she returned to his side, Mike looked up to see her smile.

"Her fever is down."

"Thank God," Mike whispered. "Earl said the weather is supposed to break by tomorrow night and finally the road to the highway will be cleared."

Andrea sighed deeply. "I sure hope so. Every time we have a wind like this, I'm afraid. Now I'm so scared that something might be wrong with Zoe that we won't be able to treat, and…"

Mike placed his arms around Andrea and held her close. "Don't even think it. It's only an old wives' tale. Zoe will be fine. By tomorrow night she'll have been seen by a doctor at the hospital, and be on her way back home."

Andrea wasn't calmed by Mike's assurance, and he knew it. His words were hollow and tinged with a confidence that he didn't feel either.

"I don't know, Mike. If we get her to Lebanon, I want her to stay there until we can be certain that she's healed."

Mike laughed a little, trying to ease the tension.

"Well, then, we can ask the neighbors to watch our house so we can stay with her till she's released."

Andrea didn't smile. She was tired, having been up with Zoe every night for the last week. Mike had offered to relieve her, but even with his help, Andrea wasn't able to sleep.

Mike sensed the tension his wife felt. "I'm sorry, honey. I was just trying to ease the pressure a bit." He took a deep breath and sighed. "I agree. If we're able to get to Lebanon tomorrow, we'll stay until Zoe has a clean bill of health."

Andrea said nothing but smiled weakly and nodded.

CHAPTER

TWO

The morning dawned gray and overcast. The snow had stopped, but the pristine mountains, snow blown by the wind, blocked every reasonable path into and out of town.

Mike turned on the television and sought a channel with a weather report. When at last he was able to find a station that was broadcasting the local weather, he turned up the volume and sat down.

"–and gale force winds battered most of northern New Hampshire, closing roads and knocking down power lines. The Department of Transportation spokesman Don Barker joins us live from Concord. Hello, Don."

The camera image switched to a man standing near the Capital Building in Concord, the wind buffeting his hair and causing him to brace against its pressure.

"Hello, Erik," the spokesman began solemnly. "It looks like we're in for a rough go. Highway crews on Route 89 have been working for nearly twenty-four hours with very little progress. Their attempts to keep the highway open have been hampered by high winds and blowing snow. The forecast is not favorable for this part of the state with new snow predicted, and gusts remaining strong."

"Don, when do you expect the roads to be passable?"

The spokesman shook his head. "That's a good question, Erik. If we don't get hit too hard, we may have a passable situation in forty-eight hours. If the wind picks up again, your guess is as good as mine."

The screen returned to the studio feed. Newscaster Erik Eckland turned to face the camera once again. "We'll have an update on the weather after this brief message, and folks, it doesn't look like it's time to put your snow shovels away for the year. We'll be right back."

A commercial for an inexpensive flight to Florida came on the screen, and Mike muted the sound.

Just what we need, he thought, *more snow and*

more wind. What we really need is to be on that plane to Florida.

Andrea walked out of Zoe's room and stood behind him, catching the last statement before the commercial.

"So, what do we do?"

Mike sighed deeply. "Well, I'm going to call Roger at the Sheriff's office and see if he knows something the newsboys don't."

The fear in Andrea's voice was only slightly veiled. "And if he doesn't?"

Mike shrugged. "If he doesn't, then we'll have to try something else."

"Like what?"

Mike stood up and gave Andrea a hug. "I'll go talk to the wind and tell it to knock it off. Even the wind can't want to keep someone as precious as Zoe from getting well."

"Actually," Andrea began, "she's doing better. She slept all night. But, I'm worried. If the roads stay closed until Monday, there won't be any medicine in town. If she gets worse, then what'll we do?"

He tried to calm Andrea's fears. "Honey, let's take this one step at a time. We may be worrying for nothing." Mike picked up the phone. "Let's see what Roger has to say."

The phone rang again and again, without answer. Just as Mike was about to hang up, a familiar voice came on the line.

"Westerhouse."

"Roger? It's Mike Wilson."

After a short exchange of greetings, Mike got right to the point.

"We've got a problem. Zoe is sick and I'm trying to find out if there's a road open between here and Lebanon. Doc Wells isn't sure what's wrong with her and she wants to get her to a hospital where there's a lab and readily available treatment."

The deputy was silent for a moment before answering. "Mike, the road situation is as bad as I've seen it since I've been here. We had to send a rescue helicopter to pick up a plowing crew that got stranded on Highway 4. Let me make a few calls, and I'll get back to you."

Mike hung up the phone and relayed the information to Andrea.

"It doesn't sound good," she said hopelessly.

Mike nodded. "Well, at least not for now. Fortunately, we've got an early start on it. Things can change a lot in a few hours. I'm gonna check with the doc and see if she can call in a prescription to a nearby pharmacy that does have the medicine. Maybe there's some in Grafton. If there is, I'll borrow Derek's snowmobile and drive over."

Andrea shook her head. "Mike, that's more than ten miles one way. You could run out of gas, or freeze–" Andrea's voice trailed off.

"Relax, Honey. I won't go unless it's our last choice. Besides, we drive more than fifty miles when we run the trails."

Andrea was undeterred. "Not in this weather we don't."

She was right and Mike knew it. However, this was not the time to show fear or hesitation. If Zoe needed the medicine, he would go, even if he had to walk.

"It'll be okay. I promise."

A short phone call to the doctor's office brought information that the nearest supply of antibiotics was in Danbury, nearly twenty miles away. That would be a push even on a very good snowmobile. The uncertainty of the terrain and the weather made such a lengthy excursion very risky.

Andrea would veto the trip if she knew where Mike was going. He decided that if Roger couldn't offer help, he would keep his destination to himself and head out while the weather was reasonable and the medicine was still on hand. However, when he approached Andrea with his plan, he realized the truth about his whereabouts was critically important. He pleaded with her over the need to get the medicine while it was still available and to his surprise, Andrea agreed.

As a precaution, Mike called his friend Derek Patterson. Derek had one of the newest and fastest snowmobiles in town. He constantly maintained it, guaranteeing that Mike would be able to make the run to Danbury with confidence; at least if the weather cooperated.

Once the arrangements were made, Mike poured himself a cup of coffee and waited for Roger's call. Andrea busied herself in the kitchen while Mike watched television for updated weather information. Current conditions did not look promising. A new front was moving in from the east, which meant moisture, and snow. Mike could not afford more snow if he were going to undertake such a long trip.

At twenty minutes after ten, the phone rang. It was Roger.

"Mike, I've got bad news. As it sits now, and probably for the rest of the daylight hours, the only way you could get Zoe to Lebanon is by helicopter."

"I was afraid you'd say that. I realize this is a stupid question, but do you think there's any possibility of that happening?"

Roger was silent for a moment before answering. "Mike, unless there is an immediate threat to Zoe's life, the chances are extremely small."

"Doc Wells is concerned. Isn't that enough?"

"Not in this weather, Mike. Concerned, is not necessarily life-threatening. Besides, we would have to free up a chopper and bring it down from Concord. The weather might break before we could get it arranged."

"Do you think there's a possibility the weather might break?"

Roger chuckled a bit on the other end of the phone.

"Mike, you've lived here longer than I have. You know the weather is absolutely unpredictable, but they said after the snowstorm blows through here tonight, we should get four or five days of clear weather. That should be soon enough to help Zoe. If it doesn't clear like they said I'll personally call the Coast Guard and see if they can help."

Mike thanked Roger and hung up the phone. Andrea had been listening quietly, saying nothing. Mike turned to face her. "Honey, you'd better make me a thermos of coffee."

Andrea appeared nervous. "Mike, she's doing better. Maybe we should wait."

Mike stood and headed to the coat closet. "And if she takes a turn for the worse and we're out of medicine, then what? No, Honey, I've gotta go. If she gets better or the weather clears in the meantime, we'll just have extra antibiotics on hand. Now, will you make me that coffee?"

Andrea turned to head for the kitchen, and Mike grabbed his phone, calling Doc Wells to arrange for the pick-up in Danbury.

"You're not actually going to take a snowmobile all the way to Danbury, are you?"

"Unless you have a helicopter that can take Zoe to Lebanon, I am. I don't have much of a choice."

Mike figured it would take over an hour to get to Danbury, that is if the weather held. He had allowed himself nearly two hours each way to make the trip. If things went as planned, he would be back before the sun went down.

CHAPTER
THREE

The weather had stayed constant, with winds and drifting flurries. As Mike drove over the deep snow, the Arctic Cat hummed at a comfortable speed of twenty-five miles an hour. The potential of hitting a deep drift or a snow rut prohibited a more aggressive drive. All Mike wanted to do was get there, get the medicine, and return home before it got dark, or the weather changed. In just over an hour, Mike pulled the snowmobile in front of the Danbury Family Pharmacy. If the return trip is as easy as this, he thought, I'll be home in no time.

The store was warm and well-lit. Mike opened his coats and walked back to the pharmacy area, to his relief, the prescription was ready and waiting. If there was a plus to this whole scenario, it was that the pharmacist suggested that the medicine be kept cold. Mike was certain he would be able to comply with that request.

After a brief conversation with the pharmacist, Mike took out his phone and called Andrea. Her voice was filled with relief that he had arrived safe and sound.

"I'm gonna drink a cup of coffee, and then I'll head back. If everything goes right, I should be home in an hour or so."

Andrea's voice expressed the deep concern which she felt. "Honey, Roger called. He said the weather is blowing in real heavy and that we may even get blizzard conditions before dark. Please hurry home, and be careful."

Mike was relieved that Andrea knew where he was. His original plan to keep his destination a secret now seemed like a bad idea.

After only a few sips of coffee, Mike checked the gas tank, warmed the engine, and headed the snowmobile back in the direction of Canaan.

Mike had a funny feeling about the return trip. Was it a forbearance? Everything had gone well. The weather had cooperated, the snowmobile was purring, and the prescription was ready. Was it possible that Zoe's condition had taken a turn? Mike pressed harder on the gas lever.

As he drove in the solitude of the barren roadway, Mike thought about Zoe. She reminded him a lot of a famous childhood star; smart, creative, and expressive. At eight years old, she was an only child and the apple of their eye. *I would have walked all the way here if I had to*, he thought. *No, I would have crawled on my hands and knees, if I had to*. He pushed still harder on the gas.

The clouds had become ominous, seeming darker and lower in the sky. The wind increased in intensity as he faced gust after gust, each blast causing the heavy machine to shutter and slow.

With only a short way to go, Mike began to see snowflakes, and the wind once again began to pound against his body and the snowmobile. Drifts that hadn't existed on his trip to Danbury now began to form along his path, making it difficult to see. Mike turned on the headlight and yelled at the wind, "Not now, damn it. Wait ten minutes, will ya?"

The streetlights on Highway 4 heading into Canaan cast an eerie glow on the unblemished snow covering the road. The only noise to be heard, other than the snowmobile, was the wind. Houses on the outskirts of town sat picturesque; their windows aglow against the forming darkness, their chimney smoke sending signals into the sky.

Almost home, Mike thought. *Only five more minutes.* Just as Mike passed the Canaan food market, a heavy gust of wind almost blew him off the snowmobile. In his effort to keep his balance, his hand slipped off the steering bar, and he let go of the gas lever. The snowmobile died.

"Son of a bitch," Mike muttered. "Don't even think of doing this now." He reached down and hit the starter button and the engine coughed but didn't start. "Not now, dammit. Not now," he repeated.

The wind had begun blowing in earnest, its gusts buffeting Mike as he sat astride the snow-mobile trying to get it re-started. His efforts seemed futile and he began considering the two miles that he would have to walk if the machine didn't start. Just when it appeared that the battery would run down, the engine seemed to catch, and slowly sputtered to a smooth idle.

Mike let out a sigh of relief. "Come on, baby, only two more miles to go. I promise, if you get me home, I'll have Derek give you an oil change and a lube job. But please, just get me there."

Darkness was closing in fast. Mike's thought that he would be home in an hour was history. It had been more than two, and he still had a bit to go. He hoped that Andrea wasn't worrying.

To his great relief, the turnoff to Castleview Lane finally arrived. The sight of his familiar neighborhood lifted Mike's spirits. He squeezed the gas lever harder and sped toward the end of the street.

In only minutes the Arctic Cat was returned to Derek's carport. Mike knocked on his door. After a brief explanation of the trip and a sincere thank you, Mike walked the short distance to the security of his own home.

Andrea was waiting with open arms. "I was starting to get worried."

Mike responded as he held her close. "I was, too. I'm sure glad to be here now."

"I can't believe you made it all the way to Danbury and back in this weather."

Mike finished pulling off his snow boots before giving her the details of his journey. "The return trip was a rough ride. The snowmobile even broke down a couple miles from home."

"What happened?"

"The engine stalled, but fortunately it restarted."

Mike set the boots near the door, took the blue and white prescription bag from the pocket of his parka, and headed toward the kitchen to place it in the refrigerator. Andrea followed and poured him a cup of coffee from the pot she had ready.

After taking a sip and then gripping the sides to warm his hands, he remarked, "At least you knew what route I was taking. If anything happened, someone would have come and found me."

"And then what?"

He sighed. "Honey, it was a trip that had to be made. Zoe needs this medicine. I didn't have a choice. I'm just glad you didn't try to talk me out of it."

Andrea stared into his eyes. She realized the gravity of the situation, and if their roles were reversed, she, too, would have driven to Danbury for the medicine.

"Well, at least you're safe now," she declared.

"And now Zoe has a few days' worth of medicine. How's she doing?"

For the first time since Mike returned, Andrea smiled. "She's doing well enough to want to see her dad."

Mike and Andrea walked into the cozy bedroom. The small blonde-haired girl rolled onto her back and smiled.

"Daddy," she said, reaching her arms up to him.

Mike walked over and picked her up, hugging her tightly. Zoe wrapped her arms around his neck and her legs around his waist before burying her face into his chest. Tears of joy welled in his eyes.

Mike couldn't help but notice that despite Andrea's encouraging words, Zoe still felt warm.

"How are you feeling, Sunshine?" He asked.

Zoe lifted her head slightly. "Sleepy," she answered through slitted eyes. My head doesn't hurt as much though." Zoe smiled slightly. "Can I have some ice cream?"

Mike and Andrea laughed. "She's definitely feeling better," Andrea said. "You get back under the covers and I'll get you a bowl."

Zoe's eyes came awake. And she leaned back against Mike's arms and clapped her hands, "Goodie," she said drawing out the word.

"Now, back in bed with you." Mike gently laid Zoe back in and covered her up. "We don't want you to catch a chill."

Zoe snuggled in under the covers, pulling them up under her chin. "Daddy?"

"What honey?"

"Am I going to die?'

Mike caught his breath, sat next to her on the edge of the bed, and did his best to appear calm. "No, honey, of course not. Why would you think that?"

"The voice told me I was."

"Who told you?" Mike asked.

"The person who controls the wind. They said it was my time to be sacrificed. What does sacrificed mean?"

Mike's heart was racing. All the talk about the power of the wind came back to mind. It wasn't an old wives' tale; it was real. He again fought his emotions to remain calm.

"We'll talk about it another time, honey. Now, it's time for some ice cream."

Andrea walked into the room at the end of their conversation.

"Talk about what later?"

"I'll tell you in a few minutes. For now, Zoe says 'I want ice cream, and I want it now'."

All of them laughed as Andrea handed Zoe the small bowl. Zoe took the spoon and dug into the creamy treat.

"I like vanilla," she said, closing her lips around another spoonful.

After a few moments, the bowl was empty and the sides scraped free of any remaining ice cream. Zoe handed the bowl to her mom and lay back down on the pillow.

"Can I take a nap now?"

Mike reached down and tucked her in. "Of course you can, sweetheart. When you wake up, if you'd like, I can read you a story."

Zoe had already closed her eyes but smiled broadly.

In only a minute, Zoe's rhythmic breathing indicated she was off to dreamland. Mike rested his hand on her forehead, saying a silent prayer before rising and walking out. Andrea followed close behind.

When they reached the door, Mike motioned with his head to Andrea to follow him, and then pulled the door almost closed. They walked into the kitchen, filled their cups with coffee, and sat down at the table.

"She looks better," Andrea said.

Mike nodded. "Her temperature's lower. That's a good sign." He took a sip of coffee.

Andrea noticed the perplexed look on Mike's face. "What is it?"

Mike shook his head and shrugged.

Andrea urged, "Just tell me."

"When you were getting the ice cream, Zoe told me she had talked to the person who was in charge of the wind. The voice told her that she was going to be sacrificed."

Andrea placed her hand over her mouth, a look of panic spread across her face.

Mike continued. "I told her not to worry and that we'd talk about it later." He took another sip of coffee and a long breath. "Everyone says it's an old wives' tale. If it is, how did she find out about it?"

Andrea's stare remained fixed on the table top, her mind focused on the possibilities that lay ahead. Tears welled in her eyes as she pleaded. "We've got to keep her fever down and get her away from here at the earliest possible second."

Andrea looked at Mike with tears rolling down her cheeks.

He took a tissue from the box, wiped her

tears, and stated, "I'm going to go out and clean the driveway. Even if it snows, I'll be further ahead. It'll be one less thing to do before we leave. Just keep the coffee hot and keep checking the weather."

Mike walked to the coat rack and put on his parka. He slipped on his boots, wrapped his scarf snugly around his neck, grabbed his gloves, turned on the outside lights, and stepped into the cold.

The wind had picked up considerably and was still blowing out of the east. Flakes continued to fall at a steady rate with the new snow collecting on top of the already-covered driveway. *Better to get started now before it gets too deep,* he thought.

FOUR

Mike's attitude was resolute as he walked to the five-gallon gas can near the garage. As was his custom, he tapped on the side of the can. The tap returned a dull thud, indicating the can was nearly full. Good, he thought. I'll stay out here until it quits snowing. Then we'll be ready to go. Because of the uncertain weather conditions, Mike had backed his Jeep into the garage. To ensure that they didn't get stranded without fuel, he would need to strap the gas can onto the back of the vehicle before they left. For now, the driveway needed his undivided attention.

Entering the garage through the side door, he flipped on the light switch and walked to where the large snow-blower stood in the front corner. Again, he checked the gas tank. A tap on the side confirmed it was also full. Mike opened the main garage door to allow himself to move the snow-blower outside.

In this neck of the woods, a well-running snow-blower was a necessity. Mike hit the starter switch and the machine sprang to life. After allowing the engine to warm, he squeezed the safety lever and guided the snow-blower into the drift in front of the garage door, clicking the auger lever so that snow was thrown in a huge arc off to the side. Once he cleared the entrance of the garage, he closed the main door and began his work in earnest.

"You won't win," the voice said.

Mike quickly let go, causing the blower to come to a halt. He looked around. No one was there.

Mike attempted to ignore the voice he'd heard, and once again grabbed the safety levers, causing the auger to turn and the motor to rev with the necessary increase in power.

"Ignoring me won't help. I will take her eventually. She is necessary for your survival."

This time Mike stopped. "My survival?" he shouted. "To hell, you say. If my survival is what's at stake, take me if you can."

"Oh, we can, Michael. At any time, we can."

A serious gust of wind blew across the drive, sending Mike reeling into a snow bank.

"See what I mean? Any time, Mike."

He freed himself from the snow bank and emptied the snow from his gloves. Obviously, this was a force to be reckoned with.

"Okay, maybe you can, but why me? Why *my* family?"

"Long ago, one of your ancestors made a pact," the wind whistled. "She was cowardly and thought she could trick fate, but now the time has come and you must pay. You must sacrifice."

"I am *not* cowardly. If there is some deed that caused this curse, let me free my family from it. Test me. Try me. Take me if you will, but leave Zoe alone."

Once again, the wind gusted and dropped Mike flat on his back in the middle of the partially cleared driveway, knocking the air out of him and causing him to bite his tongue. He slowly rolled onto his hands and knees, spitting blood as he stood up, gasping for breath.

"That's it. Take your anger out on me," Mike grunted.

"You, Andrea, and Zoe. You must all suffer."

"Says who?" Mike countered. "Who the hell do you think you are?"

The wind swirled briskly around Mike, creating a mini-tornado, stinging his face with ice crystals. Mike covered his face with his hands. Slowly, the wind calmed.

"I am the keeper of the wind, the judge of misdeeds. I have come to enact retribution for the transgressions of your great-great-great-grandmother, accused witch, Sibly Talbart."

Mike lowered his hands, now looking far into the darkness.

"I don't know who, or what, you're talking about. What does she have to do with me or my family?"

The throaty voice laughed. "Ignorance does not clear the debt. August 31, 1680, Sister Talbart, heavy with child at the time, pledged the life of her first-born daughter if the church could prove that she was a witch. Her trial was short and convincing. It was ordered that she be put to death as soon as her baby was delivered, but her daughter was stillborn. We believe she killed it, and as a result of her actions, her debt is still unpaid."

Mike thought for a minute, then exclaimed, "A witch? What are you talking about? They don't punish witches anymore. People are allowed to believe what they want these days. You *can't* take Zoe for a debt that someone else caused." The wind whistled around Mike. The voice was silent. "Do you hear me?" he shouted. "You can't harm us because of our beliefs. We've never even practiced witchcraft. Burning witches at the stake went out more than three hundred years ago." Again, the wind blew harder.

Mike was listening intently when he heard the porch door open.

"Mike? Are you okay?"

Andrea's voice startled him.

"Yeah, honey. I'm fine. Just taking a breather. Go back inside before you catch cold."

"Who were you talking to?" she asked.

"I'll tell you about it when I come in. Now, go inside."

Andrea reluctantly closed the door but stood in the doorway watching Mike as he clicked the snow-blower back into gear. After a few moments of watching Mike clear the area in front of the garage, she turned and went to check on Zoe.

Mike glanced at the door to be sure that Andrea had gone. "I know you can hear me," he shouted. "Did you hear what I said? You can't punish us for something our ancestor did long ago."

Silence.

Just as I thought, Mike mused. *When we were getting somewhere, you chicken out.*

The tension of the previous minutes had caused Mike to sweat profusely under his jacket. His palms were perspiring heavily, the extra moisture causing him to readjust his gloves to keep them firmly in place. The wind blew strongly, trying to chill his body. As he neared the edge of the house, a large spear of ice, which was hanging from the eave of the house, crashed to the ground, narrowly missing him.

Mike smiled. "So, you *can* hear me. Why won't you talk to me? Are you afraid?"

Mike's feet were pulled from under him, causing him to lurch forward onto the handles of the snow-blower. A sharp pain dug into his side.

"Son of a bitch." he murmured, grasping his side. "You're gonna get me ticked off in a second. I don't know how I'll fight you, but I won't let you win. Do you hear me? You can't win. I won't let you!"

Once again, the porch door opened. Andrea stood waving him in, screaming with panic in her voice. "Mike, you'd better come here."

"What is it?"

"Come inside. Hurry!" She yelled.

Mike clicked the snow-blower key to off, killing the engine, and ran to the door.

Andrea was already walking into Zoe's room. As Mike joined her, their daughter was sitting straight up in bed, staring into the distance. After a moment's silence, she slowly turned her head to stare in Mike's direction.

"Who is this person?" Zoe asked, the voice mellow and raspy.

Zoe's face was drawn and filled with tension.

Her eyes held a blank gaze as she stared into Mike's eyes.

"His name is Mike," Andrea said. "He's Zoe's father."

Zoe slowly turned to look at her mother again. "He cannot help us. His energy is not balanced. He must remain silent. It would be better if he were to leave the room."

"What the hell is going on?" Mike demanded.

"May I go speak with him?" Andrea pleaded.

"As you wish. Time is short. Do not tarry, lest the life of the little one be placed in jeopardy."

Andrea motioned with her head toward the door, then walked quickly to it. Mike followed her lead, glancing over his shoulder as they entered the kitchen.

"Please tell me now, what's going on with Zoe?" he implored.

Andrea stood there trembling with tears rolling down her cheeks as she searched for the right words to begin the conversation. "Zoe says there's a spirit controlling her. I think she's possessed. The voice told me her name is Sibly Talbart. She claims she's the only one who can stop the wind."

Mike gulped and his eyes grew wide. "I know that name. She's my great-great-great grandma. I've been fighting with the wind outside for more than an hour. The voice I spoke to said they are the keeper of the wind, judge of misdeeds, and that they were sent to gain restitution for some promise Sibly made hundreds of years ago."

Andrea almost fainted, but Mike caught her and helped her into one of the kitchen chairs. "You don't believe that, do you?"

Mike shook his head, taking a seat in an adjacent chair. "I don't know what to believe. There's enough stuff going on that I'm afraid to just dismiss any of it. I know I had a conversation with the wind." Mike paused for a minute, thinking. "I also can't forget the things everyone says are old wives' tales. I think there's more to it than anyone wants to let on. If we're wrong and there's nothing going on, it won't hurt us. If we're right and it's all real…" Mike's voice trailed off as he looked down. "I don't wanna go there."

"I'm really scared Mike. What should we do?" Andrea asked biting her lip.

"I think you should go back to Zoe and talk to my grandma, and I'll try to reason with the wind. In the end, we need to let the two of them fight it out," he replied.

"You mean, your grandma and the wind?"

Mike nodded, "Since Sibly seems to be our only hope, I'll honor her request… for now. Even though I want to be in the room with you and Zoe, I'll go outside and clear the rest of the drifts in the driveway, then pack the car. We can take

Zoe to Lebanon as soon as I'm finished. I'll make sure we get there."

"How? Have you seen the weather?" Andrea remarked.

His face took on an air of confidence. "Seen it and felt it," he said, touching his fingers to his mouth. "If these two can't work it out, then I would rather die trying to get her help than leave her here under the power of some ancient bounty hunter."

Andrea nodded weakly. "Maybe you're right. Will you fix some sandwiches and coffee for the ride while I see what Sibly has in mind?" Andrea stood up to return to the bedroom. "I'm not sure I can handle this much longer. If they aren't going to leave Zoe alone, then you're right, we must take matters into our own hands." She turned and disappeared around the corner. Mike reloaded the coffee pot and started making sandwiches to keep his mind off what was happening in the bedroom.

Mike's thoughts wandered. *Witches. Curses. Possession. Why had this happened? How were the deaths of the others in the past related to us?* It seemed totally illogical. Yet, with what had been going on in the past few days, Mike couldn't discount anything.

Mike had dabbled in the occult as a young man but had never crossed the line into witchcraft. In recent years, he had studied many different religions and had released the stigma, which is still held by many, regarding witches and pagans. Still, as he searched his memory, he could recall nothing in his family history about any of this.

Some time ago, he had seen a movie with a similar plot. In the film, a curse was placed on a family. From then on, all the male members faced an early death. The only way to free them from the hex was to bring in another sorcerer to erase the spell. It sounded like a dark version of *Snow White and the Seven Dwarfs* –just one kiss and the curse would be lifted.

Those were only stories. They couldn't be true, but something was definitely going on. Mike could still taste the blood in his mouth. *That was not a story*. Was it possible they'd stumbled onto the cause of all the untimely deaths which had occurred in Canaan in the past?

Mike finished the sandwiches and coffee and went to the closet to get the heavy blankets that would keep them warm should their plan go astray. *Lebanon, or bust,* he thought. *I should have done this days ago.*

With the supplies stacked on the kitchen table, Mike put on his parka and stepped back into the cold. His feet were sliding despite the special grips on the bottom of his boots. It was as though the wind was trying to cause him to lose his footing again. Mike smiled. *Not this time,* he thought. *This time, I'm going to finish the job, and then we'll be on the road.*

Before Mike restarted the snow-blower, he strapped the can of gas to the back of their Jeep and securely fastened the snow chains to the rear wheels of the vehicle. With these tasks complete, Mike stood and rested his hands on his hips, surveying the new snow on the remainder of the driveway. It was at least six inches deep, and the snow was still falling. He slowly shook his head. I don't care, he thought, reviewing the dangers of their venture in his mind. We are going to make it.

The snow-blower roared to life, idling smooth and strong. Mike clicked the machine into gear. The snow flew into a high arc, creating a pile alongside the side. After only a few minutes, it was clear, and Mike was plowing the snow away from the driveway entrance. Now, if they had to go, they were ready.

With the snow-blower once again secured in the garage, Mike closed the main door, turned out the light, and walked to the house. Just before he reached the stairs to the small back porch, a cloud of snow blew up in front of him blocking his view and causing him to stop and turn away. A loud screech preceded the violent gust of wind that hit him from behind, knocking him face down into the snow. For a moment, he lay stunned, bordering on unconsciousness. As with the previous encounter, he rose to his hands and knees and rested, catching his breath. After a couple minutes, Mike stood and resumed his walk to the house.

Damn wind, he thought. Mike burst out into laughter. "You can't have her, and now, you can't have me, either. As God is my witness, you will not win!" Again, laughter, this time followed by a glob of blood-laced phlegm being spit into the white snow beneath him. "You're mad because you can't win. Ha-ha-ha-ha-ha. You can't win. God? Do you hear me? Please help us. Break this curse. Clean this hex. Let my daughter live. After all these years and all these lives, free us from this wickedness."

The wind howled in answer, blowing loud and strong. Mike hadn't heard the crack that released the dead branch from the tall Cottonwood tree next to the house. He did feel the impact, as the falling timber crashed across the back of his head, knocking him unconscious.

CHAPTER
FIVE

"Mike? Mike? Are you alright?"

It was Andrea.

Mike lay on his back in the middle of the kitchen floor, staring into the light above the table.

He nodded. "I think so. What happened?"

Derek responded. "A branch from the tree hit you. You were out like a light."

Mike's mind began to clear. "What time is it? How's Zoe?"

"It's ten o'clock at night. Zoe's fine," Andrea reassured him.

"Is her fever still down?"

"Fever? What fever? Andrea asked. "She's sleeping. I didn't want to wake her unless we had to leave to take you to the doctor."

Mike sat up, gingerly touching the back of his head where the branch had struck him. "Well, we'd better get her up now if we're going to make it to Lebanon."

"Lebanon?" Derek and Andrea said in unison.

"Why in the world would we be going to Lebanon?" Andrea asked.

"To get Zoe to the hospital…to get antibiotics, to fight the curse of the wind."

Derek laughed. "I told you, Andrea. It must have been a pretty hard bump on the head. You might want to get it checked in the morning. His eyes are clear, so I don't think he has a concussion, but he still seems to be hallucinating. You'd better get Doc Wells to check him out."

Mike was confused. "But, what about the wind and grandma Sibly?"

Again, Andrea and Derek looked at each other before speaking in unison. "Who?"

"My great-great-great grandma Talbart, who was helping us fight the wind."

"Derek, help me get him into a chair. I'll get him some water and call the Doc. Maybe she can come over tonight."

Mike felt a tingling that ran down his arms and into the tips of his fingers almost causing him to pass out again. He took a deep breath and kept his composure.

"Zoe's not sick?" He mumbled.

Andrea sat the glass of cool water on the table next to where Mike sat and shook her head. "Not unless something happened to her in the last half hour. Why do you think she's sick?"

Again, dizziness surrounded Mike and he lay his head down on his arms, resting on the table. "It was real," he muttered. "I know it was real."

Derek laughed, handing Mike a cool damp towel. "Put this on the back of your neck. You'll feel better. Andrea, you'd better make that call."

Mike looked pleadingly at both of them. "It was the wind," he said seriously. "The wind was sent to serve judgment for a commitment Sibly made hundreds of years ago.

Once again Derek and Andrea shared a glance.

"Just rest for a while, honey," Andrea said. "You'll start feeling better in a few minutes."

Outside, the wind was calm, and the air was crisp. The moonlight glistened off the top of the powder, creating a beauty that can only be found on the eve of a snowy night. The moon's reflection was bright, and clearly lit the path that Mike followed on his way to the wood-box next to the garage. His trip to get more logs for the fireplace, nearly three hours earlier, was interrupted when he was struck by the falling limb.

Mike's head began to clear. He thought of the vision he had experienced. Was it possible it was all a dream? How could it be, if he wasn't asleep? Nothing seemed logical. He was certain that he'd been to Danbury. He knew it. He remembered the ride.

Andrea called Doc Wells and after several questions for both of them, she said there didn't seem to be an immediate worry, but asked that Mike stop in early the next day for a check-up.

In the morning, Mike did feel much better. After several cups of hot coffee, he decided to use the snow-blower to clear the snow from the driveway before heading to the doctor's office. *When that was complete,* he thought, *he would take the chainsaw and cut up the large branch that had fallen from the tree.* Mike reasoned that it was odd the branch would fall at precisely the time he was on his way to get more wood. It was probably just a strange coincidence.

Once Mike had donned his cold weather gear, he walked to the garage, entering from the side door. Turning on the light, he walked to the front corner where the snow-blower stood. In these parts of the country, a well-running machine was an absolute necessity. As was his custom, he tapped on the side of the snow-blower's tank to see how much gas it held. The drum-like echo indicated it was nearly empty. *That's odd*, he thought. *I always keep it full. How could it be empty if I hadn't run it?* Mike didn't dwell on it too much. He just chalked it up to the unusual events of last night. When he went to where he normally kept the gas can, it wasn't there. Instead, it was strapped to the back of the Jeep.

It seemed strange, but he shrugged it off and continued about his task. After filling the snow-blower with fuel, he clicked the opener. When the garage door went up, Mike stood gazing at the cleared driveway. *How did I not notice that*, he thought. Then muttered to himself, "The blower, the can, and now this. Andrea said the battle with the wind never happened."

Just then, Andrea opened the door and called out, "Mike, Zoe's up, come on in for breakfast." Zoe appeared and waved eagerly at her dad.

Is it possible the events of the prior evening were really figments of his imagination? As Mike scanned the yard in disbelief, his eyes focused on the drifts which had been blown by the rare and violent wind of the previous night.

Thank you for reading *The Wind*. We hope you enjoyed it! If you'd like to continue The Starlite

Supernatural Mystery Series, you can read our standalone shorts in any order.

Find All Our Books
linktr.ee/RayandMicheleFraser

BOOKS 2 READ

https://books2read.com/MicheleFraser

Author Notes

Thank you for reading our story.
We love hearing your feedback, so we hope you'll post a review.

~

If you liked *The Wind*, please check out our other Starlite Mysteries.

Receive an exciting look into *Mary* by signing up for our newsletter using the Bookfunnel link below.
https://dl.bookfunnel.com/xpkhinq30n

Plus, get behind the scenes tidbits and learn about new releases.

~

Mary
A young girl with a mysterious background sets off an investigation into the dark reaches of time.

Reviews

Mary

"A short paranormal novella that's just about ninety pages long: I enjoyed every aspect of it. I wished it was longer, but just because I loved the writing style - the characters. The flow of the book was just perfection. Also, I liked the action part at the beginning and the mystery each chapter brought. It never had a dull moment."
- Midnightstorybook

Mary

"Every time I thought I had an idea of who Mary was and where she came from, I'd learn about new piece of the puzzle and have to throw all my theories out the window. Things get stranger as the story progresses, which just made me more eager to figure out what was really going on. I felt a bit bad for our main character Jason and his quest to return Mary to her family, but I admired how determined he was to help such an odd little girl.

For such a brief story, "Mary" is packed full of intrigue and mystery - who is this little girl, where is she from, and why doesn't she understand how to drink a milkshake? I can guarantee you won't see the answer coming!

I really enjoyed this read, and I'd recommend it to anyone looking for a novella that will keep them guessing. I'm looking forward to reading more by Ray and Michele Fraser - thank you so much to the authors for the opportunity to read this book!"
- Anna

Mary
"Read it as an ARC. Absolutely loved this story. Held my attention the whole time. The plot was consistent from beginning to end. Gave off a murder mystery vibe without murder. No cliffhangers with a great unexpected ending. Suspenseful and mysterious. Definitely worth reading if you want to try out the supernatural mystery genre."
- Elizabeth S.

ALSO BY RAY & MICHELE

If you enjoyed this Starlite Mystery, check out our other unique spellbinding shorts. They're the perfect escape when you're pressed for time.

The Starlite Supernatural Mystery Series:

Haunted

The Wind

The Promise

Mary

1421 Maple

Sarah

Coming Soon

Enter the web of intrigue, suspense, and danger in

The Sean Thomas Paranormal Mystery Series

Book 1 - *A Switch in Time*

For a complete list of Ray and Michele's books

or

to request signed paperbacks visit our website.

www.rayandmichelefraser.com

Find All Our Books
linktr.ee/RayandMicheleFraser

BOOKS 2 READ

https://books2read.com/MicheleFraser

About the Authors

Ray and Michele are a full-time writing team with a serious passion for storytelling. They combine their love of writing, vivid imagination, and years of experience as professional spirit mediums to guide their readers into uncharted territories.

In 1994, Ray's intuitions fostered by Cherokee and Scottish ancestry, led him to open Mystiques-West Metaphysical Center in Michigan. During the twenty-three years of operation, Ray hosted a #1 radio talk show and a live TV show, called "The Mystical Connection." They performed home cleansing, organized ghost hunts, taught classes in mediumship, and led weekly public seances to connect clients to their departed loved ones on the other side. The messages from spirit have helped many to find peace. Ray also facilitated the last four National Houdini Seances sponsored by Houdini historian Sid Radner.

In addition to readings and life coaching sessions, Ray's work as an ordained minister has provided his clientele with years of grief and re-lationship counseling, weddings, and funerals.

As a screenwriter, Michele brings her love of film into the fold by incorporating her own style of creativity into their endeavors. She's also the backbone of the editing process, social media management, cover design, and marketing.

Ray and Michele infuse their stories with mystery, intrigue, tales of the afterlife, and other worldly phenomena to create a fascinating and adventurous journey for readers.

For more info - linktr.ee/RayandMicheleFraser

Ray's extensive background and keen storytelling abilities combined with Michele's love of screenwriting and editing has made them a powerhouse duo.
www.rayandmichelefraser.com

DON'T MISS OUT

Click the button below to sign up for our fan exclusive newsletter to get behind the scenes tidbits and learn about new book releases.

There's no charge or obligation and we never sell your information.

https://rayandmichelefraser.com/newsletter

https://books2read.com/MicheleFraser

Find All Our Books
linktr.ee/RayandMicheleFraser

WHAT PEOPLE ARE SAYING

Haunted
"Ray and Michele do not disappoint. I could not put this book down. It left me wanting to know more. I'm a big fan of haunted houses and was very intrigued with this story. I honestly didn't see the story going the way it did. I actually felt as if I was there. I felt all the emotions the characters felt. I'm still in awe at the story and cannot wait until their next book!!"
- Shana L.

~

The Promise
"Just finished reading this story... and I am blessed beyond words! It's a beautiful paranormal novella focusing on grief, loss, sadness, and ultimately - redemption. For lovers of *Chicken Soup for the Soul* books and the *Sixth Sense* film, you will be delighted to have the time to read this short story - and feel compelled to engage in the entire series! Thank you to @rayandmichelefraser for the wonderful opportunity to share this story of mystery and

intrigue with you all! I highly recommend and
rate it 5 of 5 sweet stars!”
- Deb

~

Mary
“I went into this novella only knowing that it was
described as a paranormal mystery. I love
paranormal books but I don’t read mystery too
often so I was interested to see how these two
genres combined. Immediately as the story began
I was interested in discovering who exactly this
mysterious Mary was. I thought I had an idea as
to where things were going and who Mary was
but I was so wrong! I don’t want to spoil
anything, but when Jason started digging up the
past I certainly didn’t expect the story to go
where it did. This was a quick yet captivating
read that I’d recommend if you’re a fan of either
paranormal or mystery.”
- MissS3LFD3STRUKT

~

1421 Maple
"I really enjoyed this short story! It's one of those thrillers that you can finish on a lunch break and feel like you spent 45 minutes in an alternate universe. I was intrigued from the beginning, but a plot twist came around and I had to keep reading to see what was going on. Perfect for those just getting into a thriller genre!"
- Brenna P., Outreach Librarian

~

Sarah
"This is a page turner. Sarah finds herself in a destructive marriage that is not at all what she thought she was getting into. Charlie is charming on the outside with an evil heart. To survive, she had to do something drastic. But will she ever be truly free from her torturing husband? Fans of A Tell Tale Heart will find this an interesting twist on a classic story."
- Brook